# THE WISH TREE

For Jackie Kaiser
(with a very special thank you
to Chris, Victoria, and Sara) –K. M.

For Mom & Pop –C. T.

ISBN 978-1-338-25683-3

Text copyright © 2016 by Kyo Maclear.
Illustrations copyright © 2016 by Chris Turnham.
All rights reserved. Published by Scholastic Inc.,
557 Broadway, New York, NY 10012, by arrangement with
Chronicle Books LLC. SCHOLASTIC and associated logos are
trademarks and/or registered trademarks of Scholastic Inc.

12 11 10 9 8 7 6 5 4                              17 18 19 20 21 22

Printed in the U.S.A.                                          40

First Scholastic printing, October 2017

Design by Sara Gillingham Studio
Typeset in Kowalski Pro
Title type handlettered by Chris Turnham
The illustrations in this book were rendered digitally.

# The WISH TREE

WORDS BY Kyo Maclear  PICTURES BY Chris Turnham

SCHOLASTIC INC.

Charles wanted
to find a wish tree.

His brother said,
"There is no such thing."

His sister said,
"There is no such thing."

But Charles said,
"What do you think, Boggan?"

And Boggan thought, surely,
there was such a thing.

So the next morning
Charles and Boggan set forth.

His brother said,
"Bring a map."

His sister said,
"Don't forget a compass."

But Charles and Boggan were already well on their way into the woods.

"La-di-da-di-da-di-daaaa," sang Charles.

"Whishhhhh," sang Boggan.

They had the whole day ahead of them.
The whole day to find a wish tree.

Up, up to the top of a hill they climbed.

And down, down to a frosty
meadow they slid.

Where Charles went Boggan followed.
Where Boggan went Charles followed.

Charles and Boggan
did not see the wish tree.

But they did see . . .

Squirrel, who was puzzling over how to get some hazelnuts to his home.

Hold on tight.

"La-di-da-di-da-di-daaaa," sang Charles.

"Whishhhhh," sang Boggan.

Slow, slow through the snow they went.
And hush, hush, past Bear's den they crept.

Where Charles went Boggan followed.
Where Boggan went Charles followed.

They did not see a wish tree anywhere.
But they did see . . .

Beaver, who was busy
gathering birch wood
to bring to his lodge.

let's go.

"La-di-da-di-da-di-daaaa," sang Charles.

"Whishhhhh," sang Boggan.

Slide, glide, across the ice they slipped,
past a few logs and around a bend.

Where Charles went Boggan followed.
Where Boggan went Charles followed.

The wish tree was nowhere to be found.
But they did find . . .

Fox, who was late getting berries to her burrow.

"load 'em up."

"La-di-da-di-da-di-daaaa," sang Charles.

"Whishhhhh," sang Boggan.

Now they had less than half the day ahead of them.
Less than half the day to find a wish tree.

"We may need to move a little faster, Boggan," said Charles.

Charles and Boggan were moving
very slowly now. Their shadows were
growing longer. The whole day was
almost behind them.

"Boggan," Charles said, "I am tired.
I cannot. Search. Any. Longer."

"Shhhhh," whispered Boggan.

When Charles awoke it was snowing.

It was snowing on Squirrel and it was snowing on Beaver and it was snowing on Fox and it was snowing on everyone.

For a moment Charles could not see through the falling snow. But then he said, "Oh, look."

"See, Boggan?" said Charles.
"Just as we thought."

And Boggan said, "Wishhhh."

Charles wrote his wish on a piece of paper
and tied it around a branch of the wish tree.

The snow was falling more gently now. The animals
had prepared a night feast. With hazelnut soufflé, a
pot of birch tea, and biscuits made of berries.

Charles and Boggan celebrated with their
friends until it was time to be on their way.

The moon was glowing brightly.

"La-di-da-di-da-di-daaaa," sang Charles.

"Whishhhhh," sang Boggan.

All the way home.

KYO MACLEAR is a critically acclaimed novelist, essayist, and children's book author. Her books have received starred reviews, appeared on numerous "Best of" lists, and been published in multiple languages around the world. Her recent picture book *Virginia Wolf* has been adapted for stage, and her picture book *Julia, Child* is currently being adapted into an animated television series. Kyo lives in Toronto.

CHRIS TURNHAM has had a long production art career working as a visual development artist in the animation industry for clients including Sony Pictures Animation, LAIKA, and DreamWorks Animation. In addition to illustrating children's books, he spends much of his time in the studio pursuing his passion for printmaking. Chris is based in Los Angeles.